DUCK for President

Doreen Cronin

Illustrated by Betsy Lewin

Simon & Schuster Books for Young Readers

NEW YORK   LONDON   TORONTO   SYDNEY

For Cathy—*D. C.*   To life, liberty, and the pursuit of happiness—*B. L.*

Visit us at www.abdopub.com

Spotlight, a division of ABDO Publishing Company, is a school and
library distributor of high quality reinforced library bound editions.

Library bound edition © 2006

SIMON & SCHUSTER BOOKS FOR YOUNG READERS ★ An imprint of Simon & Schuster Children's Publishing Division ★
1230 Avenue of the Americas, New York, New York 10020 ★ Text copyright © 2004 by Doreen Cronin ★ Illustrations copyright
© 2004 by Betsy Lewin ★ All rights reserved, including the right of reproduction in whole or in part in any form. ★ SIMON &
SCHUSTER BOOKS FOR YOUNG READERS is a trademark of Simon & Schuster, Inc. ★ Book design by Dan Potash ★ The text for this
book is set in Filosofia. ★ The illustrations for this book are rendered in brush and watercolor.   10 9 8 7 6 5 4 3 2

Library of Congress Cataloging-in-Publication Data ★ Cronin, Doreen. ★ Duck for President / Doreen Cronin ; illustrated
by Betsy Lewin.—1st ed. ★ p. cm. ★ Summary: When Duck gets tired of working for Farmer Brown, his political ambition
eventually leads to his being elected President. ★ ISBN 0-689-86377-2 (hc) ★ 1-59961-091-4 (reinforced library bound
edition) ★ [1.Ducks—Fiction. 2. Elections—Fiction. 3. Politics, Practical.] I. Lewin, Betsy, ill. II. Title. PZ7.C88135
Du 2004 ★ [E]—dc22 ★ 2003021923

All Spotlight books are reinforced library binding and manufactured in the United States of America.

Running a farm is very hard work.

At the end of each day Farmer Brown is covered from head to toe in hay, horsehair, seeds, sprouts, feathers, filth, mud, muck, and coffee stains.

He doesn't smell very good, either.

The animals have chores to do, too.

PIGS- CLEAN UNDER THE BEDS

COWS- WEED THE GARDEN

SHEEP- SWEEP THE BARN

DUCK- TAKE OUT THE TRASH
MOW THE LAWN
GRIND COFFEE BEANS

At the end of each day
the pigs are covered in lint bunnies.
The cows are covered in weeds.
The sheep are covered in dust.

**And Duck is covered in tiny bits of grass
and espresso beans.**

Duck did not like to do chores.

He did not like picking tiny bits of grass and espresso beans out of his feathers.

"Why is Farmer Brown in charge, anyway?" thought Duck.

"What we need is an election!"

He made a sign and hung it up in the barn.

The next morning Farmer Brown found a poster on his front door.

VOTE DUCK!

For a Kinder, Gentler Farm!

Farmer Brown was furious.
He ran to the barn and found the animals
registering to vote.

The mice got together and protested the
height requirement. So Duck crossed it off.

On Election Day each of the animals filled out
a ballot and placed it in a box.
The vote was counted, and the results were
posted on the barn wall.

Farmer Brown demanded a recount.

One sticky ballot was found
stuck to the bottom of a pig.

The new tally was:

F. BROWN 6
DUCK   21

The voters had spoken.

Duck was officially in charge.

Running a farm is very hard work.

At the end of each day Duck was covered from head to toe in hay, horsehair, seeds, sprouts, feathers, filth, mud, muck, and coffee stains.

"Running a farm is no fun at all," thought Duck.

That night Duck and his staff started working
on Duck's campaign for governor.

Duck left Farmer Brown in charge and hit the campaign trail.

He visited small-town diners.

He marched in parades.

He went to town meetings.

He gave speeches that only other ducks could understand.

On Election Day the voters filled out their ballots in booths all over the state.

The vote was counted, and the results were posted in the local paper.

The governor demanded a recount.

Two sticky ballots were found stuck to
the bottom of a plate of pancakes.

The new tally was:

MS. Governor
299,999

DUCK 300,002

The voters had spoken.

Duck was officially in charge.

Running a state is very hard work.

At the end of each day Duck was covered from head to toe in hair spray, ink stains, Scotch tape, fingerprints, mayonnaise, and coffee stains.

And he had a very bad headache.

"Running a state is no fun at all," thought Duck.

That night Duck and his staff started working on posters for the presidential election.

Duck left his staff in charge and hit the campaign trail.

He kissed babies in local diners.

He rode in parades.

He gave speeches that only
other ducks could understand.

He even played the saxophone on late-night television.

On Election Day the voters filled out their ballots in booths all over the country.

The vote was counted, and the results were announced on CNN.

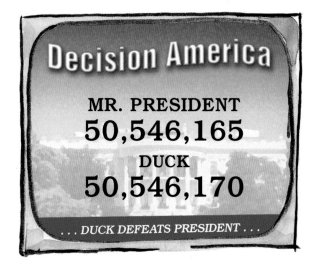

Decision America

MR. PRESIDENT
50,546,165
DUCK
50,546,170

. . . DUCK DEFEATS PRESIDENT . . .

The president demanded a recount.

Ten sticky ballots were found stuck to the bottom of the vice president.

The new tally was:

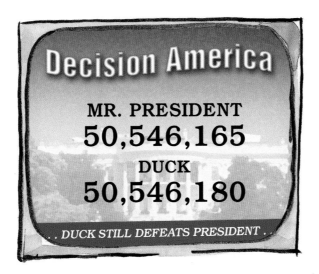

Decision America

MR. PRESIDENT
50,546,165
DUCK
50,546,180

. . DUCK STILL DEFEATS PRESIDENT . .

The voters had spoken. Duck was officially in charge.

Running a country
is very hard work.

At the end of each day
Duck was covered from
head to toe in face powder,
paper cuts, staples,
security badges,
Secret Service agents,
and coffee stains.

And he had a very bad
headache.

"Running a country is no
fun at all," thought Duck.

Then he checked the help-wanted ads.

★ DUCK NEEDED ★
No experience necessary.
Must be able to mow the lawn
and grind coffee beans.

Duck left the vice president in charge
and headed back to the farm.

At the end of each day Farmer Brown is now covered
from head to toe in hay, horsehair, seeds, sprouts,
feathers, filth, mud, muck, and coffee stains.

And Duck . . .

. . . is working on his autobiography.